Thoughtsfull

By Chi

Order this book online at www.trafford.com
or email orders@trafford.com

Most Trafford titles are also available at major online book retailers.

Printed in Victoria, BC, Canada.

ISBN: 978-1-4269-1549-9

*Our mission is to efficiently provide the world's finest, most comprehensive book
publishing service, enabling every author to experience success. To find out how
to publish your book, your way, and have it available worldwide, visit us online
at www.trafford.com*

Trafford rev. 4/1/2010

 www.trafford.com

North America & international
toll-free: 1 888 232 4444 (USA & Canada)
phone: 250 383 6864 ♦ fax: 812 355 4082

**For He that has
walks with me...**

Life   Love   Spirit   Me

Contents Page

Life

Thoughtsfull

Life   *Love*   *Spirit*   *Me*

Life   Love   Spirit   Me

Thoughtsfull

Life   *Love*   *Spirit*   *Me*

Life   Love   Spirit   Me

Thoughtsfull

Life   *Love*   *Spirit*   *Me*

Life   Love   Spirit   Me

Words are...

A writer's music
An ignorant's lesson
A rapper's hope
A poet's expression...

Thoughtsfull

Life

A handful of rice

The world is a scale that is
leaning to one side
Too much weight on the
Western world and the wealth
will not divide
We are driving our 'Benz' and
flossing our 'Ice'
While babies somewhere are
crying for a handful of rice.

If you choose you lose, but what
choice was made,
By the children with the choice -
go to school or get paid.
As some girls dress in clothes so
the boys they entice
Other girls sell their bodies for a
handful of rice.

Life   Love   Spirit   Me

When things don't go our way,
we are sure to rave and rant
We get hung up over little things
at are not significant
We fight over car spaces or if
money is not precise
Yet some people are still dying
for a handful of rice.

We are quick to waste food, just
to buy again tomorrow
Because to get food we do not
beg, steal or borrow
We buy cheap for their labour
and sell at ten times the price
While we give nothing to the
people that need a handful of
rice.

We remember sometimes when
the adverts are on TV
But if the pictures is too
disturbing we may change from
channel 3
Perhaps we think about giving
money, we think that once or
twice
But by the third time we have
forgotten of the handful of rice.

Branches

There are several different paths
of branches, that will lead you to
the top of the tree,

Just because you path is
different to mine does not mean
your better than me.

Just because more people take
your path does not mean your
path is best,

I way I choose to climb the tree,
suits me in my life's quest.

Conform

You may not conform much to
the 'it girls' of today
You may not be a size 8 with hair
that is fly away.
You may not have double D
breasts and a 24 inch waist.
Any You may think fashion is a
matter of individual taste.

You may not mix well in the
clubbing scene
Bit like a cattle market, and you
don't feel prime or lean
Your clothes may not be
designer; So design my own
wear?!
And for those that don't like it,
learn not to care.

Life   Love   Spirit   Me

Just because you do not
conform, does not mean you are
not
A beautiful woman, so be secure
with what you've got.
Be a queen to yourself, truth to
yourself you owe.
You are what you are until God
says so.

You see glossy-mags illustrates a
beauty far from my own
So girls attempt to conform with
acts I cannot condone.
But when I look at myself, I am
proudly NOT like those we see.
I do not need to 'correct' this
image with 'corrective' surgery.

Society may not recognise,
because my beauty goes deeper,
I am my own provider and I am
my own keeper.
I do not rely on anyone to
recognise what is in me
Something different is not
always noticed until it's too late
to see.

So if you feel what I write, stand
proud again
You are that mighty woman that
will raise mighty children.
Don't aim to conform aim to be
happy
And start by loving yourself and
all that you see!

Getting Old

You know you're getting old,
when you start driving a bigger
car.
When you no longer play loud
music and babies leave you 'garr
- garr'.
You know you're getting old,
when family leaves far
You know you're getting old
You know you're getting old

You know you're getting old,
when you can 'understand' your
mum.
Your younger brother's height
exceeds yours and you expect
mail to come.

You know you're getting old,
when you think school was fun!
You know you're getting old.
You know you're getting old.

You know you're getting old,
when you start shopping in
'Wallis'
You can't wear the latest fashion
and young children call you
'Miss'
You know you are getting old
when your style of dressing is
'classic'!
You know you're getting old.
You know you're getting old.

You know you're getting old,
when you start thinking of your
past
You start thinking of your future
and how to make relationships
last!
You know you're getting old,
when your bills are too vast.
You know you're getting old.
You know you're getting old.

You know you're getting old,
when men don't ask your age
When you start drinking more
water and you can relate to this
page!
You know you're getting old,
when you're in denial stage.
You know you're getting old.

Life   Love   Spirit   Me

You know you're getting old.

You know you're getting old,
when you haven't been seen for
'ages'.
You listen to the news and your
love-life is going through stages.
You know you're getting old,
when you don't paid - you get
wages!
You know you're getting old.
You know, you're getting old!

Life is like a puzzle

Life is like a puzzle that you piece
together as you go along.
Sometimes, the wrong pieces of
the puzzle are put together.
These mistakes can only be
rectified when they are
recognised as wrong.
These mistakes will only be
repeated if you don't learn as
you go along.
Life is like a puzzle; think about
the pieces that fit together or
the picture may not turn out
right.

Love is like a game were
everyone has their own rules.

Life   Love   Spirit   Me

When you to play to someone
else's rules you may end up
getting hurt.
For this game has no strategies
and differs every time.
We should learn to love and to
be loved by you own rules.
Love is like a game – try not to
play it.

Your family is like your face; you
may not like it, but you are stuck
with it!
It always seems that another
person's face is better than your
own.
But there is no perfect face -
there is no perfect family,

And you do not have to like it to
love it.
Your family is like your face; look
after your face, it is the only one
you have.

Getting friends are like buying
fruits; you have to taste to know
their worth.
A dishonest friend can leave a
bitter taste, but not all apples
taste the same.
And every apple is different
depending where you buy
You may taste many bad apples
on your journey before you find
one that is sweet.
Friends are like fruits – wish we
could try before we buy.

Life   Love   Spirit   Me

God is like electricity you cannot
see but you are affected daily by
His presence
The light switches on, the kettle
boils and the fridge refrigerates
without you seeing a spark.
But you know electricity exists
because without it, things
wouldn't work.
And you know God exists
because without him, things
wouldn't work.

The strongest powers that exist
are those you cannot even see.

The fairest of them all

Mirror mirror on the wall – who
is the fairest of them all?

The West, with all the money, all
the food and the armed forces?
Or the East, with all the will (but
no way) but the natural
resources?

The West, with 'freedom of
speech', yet selected daily news.
Or the East, with no freedom,
and frustrated violence to
express views.

The West lends money to the
countries they robbed centuries
ago.
The East's rich get richer, with
poverty at an all time low.

The West, pointing the finger
east, for what they did
themselves in the past.
Whilst the East, hopes to solve
everything with one atomic
blast.

Mirror mirror on the wall – who
is the fairest of them all?

The reason for life

We all are born into this world
with the aim to be happy.
All we do in this world is so that
we can, be happy.
Our actions, good or bad, are to
ensure we will be happy
We go to church to ensure, in
the end, our spirit is happy.
This world has progressed to
show us how to be happy
This world has taught us, money
will make us happy

Anything you want can be
bought with money.
Can everything you need be
bought with money?

Life   Love   Spirit   Me

Higher quality of products;
higher amounts of money.
Higher quality of people; higher
amounts of money?!
We are roped along with the
promise of money.
At the end of the rope will we be
happy with that money?

So we start as soon as we can to
look for work.
From 16 to 60 all we do is work.
From Monday to Friday all we do
is work.
Our lives are mapped; school -
college - work.
Our monotonous day is a routine
around work

To be happy we need money and
so need to work.

So we work to get money to be
happy and enjoy life.
But this work keeps us busy we
don't have time for life
Maternity leave is one year to
raise the most important life.
Holiday- 2 weeks a year; 2 week
to live your life.
Occasionally 'something
happens' to put a prospective on
life
If that 'something' is death then
it is too late to live life.

Happy = Money=Work
=Life=Happy = Money=Work
=Life??

The Same

If everybody looked the same in
this world, then it would be a
different place
Nothing will surprise us, truly
revive us, because everyone
would have the same face.
There would no 'beautiful' or
'ugly' people, because we will all
look the same.
Our characters will define us,
that way our looks won't take
the blame.

If we all looked alike then we
might stop discriminating.

Stop looking down on those that
are different and stop people-
hating.
Young schoolgirls will stop
starving themselves to try and
get thin.
People will not be judged upon
on the tone of their skin.

But difference individualises us,
personalises us and makes us
unique.
It specialises us in this versatile
world to the partners that we
seek.

If everyone thought the same in
the world, then it would quiet
place.

Life   *Love*   *Spirit*   *Me*

No one would argue in courts
anymore because they'll all have
the same case.
The politics around this world of
ours would soon be dissolved.
Because before they get to the
bombing and fighting, problems
will be resolved.

*But if we all thought the same
then we wouldn't think anything
new.
We wouldn't be able to learn
from each other because we'll
have the same point of view.*

No matter how we hate it,
different opinions help to
broaden our minds.

Life   Love   Spirit   Me

It is the different thinking of
different people that has
developed mankind.

We may not always understand
the difference but we need to
learn to respect.
For it is the lack of this, that led
to the worlds wars and world
debt.

The Three S's

Sun

Brings about a strange euphoric
feeling.
Express healing with skin
revealing,
Seems to make you less irritated
As the days become exhilarated,
In the sun, the party' begun, with
hours of fun.
Long days and warm nights
Takes your spirit to new heights
Leave the trouble for tonight
In the sun......

Sex
Brings about a strange euphoric
feeling.
Express healing with skin
revealing,
Seems to make you less irritated
As the days become exhilarated,
When you have sex, your no
longer vex, better with your ex??
Long days and warm nights
Takes your spirit to new heights
Leave the trouble for tonight
When you have sex......

Shopping
Brings about a strange euphoric
feeling.

Express healing with new clothes
revealing,
Seems to make you less irritated
As the days become exhilarated,
When you shop, you just can't
stop, credit ratings drop
Long days and warm nights
Takes your spirit to new heights
Leave the trouble for tonight
When you shop……

We don't question why.

This world is so funny – but more
the people in it.
If we stop and question what we
do, we'll wonder why we do it!
But we don't, just follow blindly,
the blind leading the blind.
We can't see what we are
looking for and we don't know
what to find.

So many things going on in this
world and we don't question
why.
We carry on with our regular
days, and months and years go
by.

I wonder, do we ever stop just to
review the journey travelled?
Then we may get questions
answered, for in the past the
truth is unravelled.

When asked about our goal in
life is it material things we strive
for?
The job, the car, the house in
Spain, and our true goals we
ignore.
The laws of man and the law of
God may not always mix...
Would you rather be judged by
12 in this life or carried away by
6?

For there will be many days of
OKAY before there is 1 day of
utter disaster.
There may be 100 days for the
thief to steal only one day is
needed for the master.
Years of living our ignorant lives
will have to change one day.
The thief cannot keep on stealing
– there will come a time to pay.

But when that day comes for us,
on our actions we will reflect.
We won't always be asked what
we did wrong and what we did
correct.
For it's not always the things we
do but the things to others we
let slip by….

Life   Love   Spirit   Me

With all this confusion in this
world why can't we question
why?

What if?

What if there was a national
secret that was commonly
known?
What if 'The Establishment' has
bugs attached to every phone?

What if 'science fiction' is
'science fact' but we don't
believe,
Because it is told to us in an act,
so the true we don't perceive?

What if, the mentally insane are
those that know the truth?
So they are locked up so they can
all be controlled under one roof?

They say there is no smoke
without fire and through truth
comes fiction.
What if, by writing these words I
cause political friction?

If every star you see in the sky is
a potential burning Sun
Then there are millions of
potential galaxies about, and you
think we are the only ones?

What if 'X-files' are real files and
the 'Matrix' does exist?
What if, there is more to the
random numbers on your email
list?

If you were about rob a house or
invade an area hugely sought for,
Would you burst into the front
room or sneak through the back
door?

Woman

She is 16 and lives alone in one
room with her son
She is now responsible for
another young and innocent one.
She chose not to abort; for her
that was not the easy way out
In her eyes he is the only thing
that is her own without a doubt.
School – a swear word. Her
education was from the street.
She had left home early as her
eyes and her fathers could not
meet.
Her baby's daddy long time left
her with remarkable ease.
She is forced to be a woman, a
brave woman, love her please.

Life   Love   Spirit   Me

76 year-old lady, long retired
nurse.
Formally independent, before
she took a turn for the worst.
Raised a family of 3 boys all
happily married with wives.
Seems all of them are too busy
now with their 'very important'
lives
Now she's in a nursing home due
to her deterioration of health
With a nurse to change her bed
at night and each time she wets
herself.
She worked hard for a pension
that doesn't even cover the fees
But she is still a woman, a great
woman, respect her please.

Life   Love   Spirit   Me

Great job, nice house, doing the
best that she can
Doing so well for her fine self she
intimidates every man
Her bank account is full but her
heart is far from rich
And when she wants to have her
say she's a "single lonely bitch"
After hours of meeting she
comes home to a hungry cat
As she fights the tears, she's
prayed for years, she prayed for
more than that.
Beneath the grand exterior, is a
woman on her knees
She is a woman, a strong
woman, be proud of her please.

The case of the Ex

Consistently resisting the
persistent thoughts of him.
As your mind resorts to him,
weighs the longs and shorts of
him.
Always thinking of the times you
had the perfect relationship.
And when alone, go through
mimes of your romantic
courtship.
The days drag on, the weeks are
long, as you're thinking of him
for hours.
Deciding what went wrong, now
love has gone, and hurt
empowers.

Needless to say that you will
miss the sex....
But you two have had your day
in the case of the ex.

Your memory has blanked the
times were things were tough
When you'd both had enough,
and the words were a bluff.
You love him then you hate him,
then you love, then you hate.
All the words that were said by
him – the lies you contemplate.
He has lied, you have cried, till
the tears have dried - his new
girl, have you met her?

Though it hurts inside, with your
friends you confide and with
time it will get better.
Emotions are high, situations
complex.
But that is the reason why this is
the case of the ex.

Honey

My dark honey, smooth, sweet
and warm like the sun
Heaven should have warned me
how I'd feel on the day you'd
come.
I watch you when you sleep,
seem so innocent to me
You can't go back to sugar, once
you've tasted honey.

Kisses in the morning and loving
in the night.
Someone stop me, I'm falling, for
this feels so right
I look into my future and it is you
I see,

Because you can't go back to
sugar, once you've tasted honey.

I see you when I can, forever on
the phone,
This 'thang' is getting deeper,
but will my head condone?
For my heart is already gone as
far as it can be
You can't go back to sugar, once
you've tasted honey.

Your words are just as deep as
your kisses, I find.
Kisses to excite my body and
word to excite my mind.
My Intelligent man, you fascinate
me

I can't go back to sugar, now I've
tasted honey.

If you watch more what I do, not
so much what I say,
You will find my 'no' means yes,
and my 'go' means stay.
On the days I am doubtful and
question your feelings for me.
Because I can't go back to sugar,
now I've tasted honey.

But nothing lasts forever; too
much of anything is not good
Word and acts unsaid, and even
now I don't think I could.
But I would do it again even if I
could foresee.

That you can't go back to sugar,
once you've tasted honey.

Now what once brought me joy,
now brings me pain
And I forever wonder will I taste
such honey again
But I cannot cry, for my pride
long proceeds me
And I can't go back to sugar, now
I've tasted honey.

But time will heal my heart a
strong spirit will heal my soul
I will finally regain my sudden
loss-of-control.
I still love honey but now I
recognise it in me,

You can't go back to sugar, once
you've tasted honey.

It's time to call it a day.

Don't let the silly games begin
Don't let the emotional blackmail
win
Let us stop participating
Because its time to call it a day.

Let us not let the phone calls
start
With arguments of how we fell
apart
But I'm tired of your tricks of the
heart
Because it time to call it a day.

Let us make this 'amicable'
division come

What's mine, what's your and
what's second to none.
Let us get this final job done,
Because it's time to call it a day.

Today I will stop the tears
The pain of loving you for years
and years
Because you've brought to life
my worst fears
Now it's time to call it a day.

Jealousy

Hers Side

Yeah, I'm jealous. I am jealous of
them.
I'm jealous of all your other
women.
At night they call you no matter
when.
Why are women calling my man
at half past ten?!
I am your girl - you should be
about me!
Then I may not be filled with so
much jealousy.
Are they prettier than me - have
you had them in bed?
Don't answer- your actions have
all but said!

Life   Love   Spirit   Me

You came back home late – who
is that on the phone?
Don't go out with your friends –
let us stay there alone.

But only you will condone my
jealous plight?
When I get home, can I call you
tonight??

His Side

I'm not jealous just 'concerned'
about you.
That is why I always want to tell
you what to do!
Forget about the past because
now you are with me.

Life   Love   Spirit   Me

I am the Man and that's the way
it should be.
I tell you what to wear because I
know what men think.
And when they all stare, I know
what men think!

We are finished, we are through,
we're over, this is done.
For I get the growing feeling that
I'm not the only one?

But who else will condone my
jealous plight?
When I get home, can I call you
tonight??

LOVE?

You brought me into your life
and spat me back out
But I still love you.

You took control of my mind and
filled it with doubt
But I still love you.

You made promises and not one
did you keep
But I still love you.

You stood there and watched
when I was falling for you deep
But I still love you.

You made insecure what was
once confident
But I still love you.

...and when I think of all the
money I spent....
I still love you.

You slept with other girls while
you were still with me
But I still love you.

You abused my confidentiality
But I still love you.

You hit me with words that last
longer than the bruises
And I still love you.

In every fight, I am the one that
loses
But I still love you.

And when you leave me for
another young miss
I will still love you.

When our whole relationship
you dismiss
I will still love you.

When I'm alone and bitter in
years to come
I will still love you.

When it all said and done
I will still love you...

Love is not enough

I see you standing there
watching me
As you've noticed me watching
you
The attraction there sparks
instantly
We move on to round two.

We like the same music, think
the same things
We converse for hours and
hours.
Then suddenly there is much
more to this fling
And love over takes and
empowers.

The date, the engagement, the
big white wedding,
It seems there has never been a
happier time,
Does either know where we are
both heading?
Who cares when loves in its
prime?!

Now our separate lives come
together, adjusting is quite
tough,
When we find we cannot work
together that's when love is not
enough.

We plan to get a mortgage so we
can stop this high rent,

Life   Love   Spirit   Me

Just like many other plans
before,
But it would seem the money we
saved, we spent
In the end we will end up paying
much more.

Working two jobs and working
apart
I walk in as you are walking out.
Our marriage no longer based on
affaires of the heart
And I'm getting tired of running
about

Babies bring families together,
But not when the family is
already strained.
We try our best and endeavour

Life   Love   Spirit   Me

That this new entry is self-
contained.

When the red-letter bills need
paying and the kids are crying for
foodstuff
As a team we are not
functioning, that's when love is
not enough
If we had talked for just a bit
longer
If our individual plans were made
one.
Then maybe our marriage would
have been stronger
Our marriage wouldn't have
ended before we begun.

It takes more than love to work
as a team
When we have to deal with life's
tribulations
The stressful times and the
monotonous routine
Leaves love outside real-life
calculations.

When we carry love solely in our
hearts
We think for all that's empty,
love refills
But that is when the problem
starts
When discovered love cannot
pay the bills

We dreamed about romance and
love in life – it was all a bluff.
For when the honeymoon is over
love is simple not enough.

Take you there

I am not strange, just
misunderstood,
I feel the same as any other
woman would.
Living today but still affected by
the past,
If love is for real than it should
last.

I am not 'all that'- but you are
attracted to me,
Is it the way I am dressed when
we first see?
But we are friends now, and you
know me well,
Still attracted? Only time will
tell...

Life   Love   Spirit   Me

Massage my mind
Kiss my lips
Touch my soul
Feel my dips
Tickle my tummy
Play with my hair
Join my spirit
And I'll take you there.

My broad nose, my full lips
Chocolate skin and high hips
My jewel is not for all to see
Those that understand, unravel
beauty.

I won't come begging to you for
more
And I'm not a '34', '24','34'.

But my intricate style and
feminine grace
Will keep a lingering smile on
your face.

Excite my body
Excite my mind
Love all this
Don't leave it behind
Comfort my tears
And enlighten me
Because that's how a true friend
lover should be.
I'll stand behind you to catch if
you fall
We'll hold each other tight so we
both stand tall
Silence speaks more than any
words could portray

Life   Love   Spirit   Me

And I'll keep loving you although
I may not say.

When u talk to me – an instant
turn on!
Intelligent Black man your dark
days are gone!
Your articulate self with sharp
eyes to see
All that is not written but is
reality.

I can't answer all questions
When you ask why
But I'll hold u when you have the
strength to cry.

Tickle my tummy
Play with my hair

Life   *Love*   *Spirit*   *Me*

Join my spirit
And I'll take you there.

The curse

In the beginning it is told that
woman ate from the tree
forbidden by God. From that day,
God must have cursed woman,
truly he must have cursed
woman.

For every day of her life;
considered second to man
And the tears that she cries will
be related to man
The mistakes that she makes,
because she turn fool for man
She is cursed to fall fool for the
love of her man

For she will not listen even
though he is the wrong man
The fairy-tale love story?? that's
her and her man!
All the beginning faults?? – She
can change her man!
She is cursed to fall fool for the
love of her man

When a slap turns to a punch,
she will stick by her man
If she left him before, she'll go
back to her man
Going through pain just for
loving her man
She is cursed to fall fool for the
love of her man

She will love honour and obey
for he is her man
He will love honour and obey
another woman
The mother of his child but
where is her man?
She is cursed to fall fool for the
love of her man

She'll fight friends and family
over this man
Thinking he'll change if she gives
more to her man
Pregnant again...but where is her
man?
She is cursed to fall fool for the
love of her man

The culture we know pushes
woman below man
But this culture we know was
written only by man
Does God not love woman as he
loves man??
Yet she is still cursed to fall fool
for the love of her man

The One

He will be the one I talk to when
I'm down.
Sooth my mind and ease my
frown.

He will be the one that knows
me inside out
My greatest fears, my joys and
what I'm about.

He will be the one that keeps me
warm at night
Yet reduce me to tears when we
fuss and fight.

He will be the one that relaxes
me

Life   Love   Spirit   Me

In times of shock, he will be my
brandy.

He will be the drug for which my
mind and body yearn
The One that cures my 'feening'
with love and concern.

He will be my 999 in my time of
need
Just to hold me when I'm tired
and too scare to lead.

He will be my blind spot, my soft
point, and my weakness
In him a friend and lover each
one I'll love no less.

And when he is the One, I will be
his
Always, forever I will be his

Then I look at us.

I see couples walking, holding
hands in the station
I see him saying something to
make her laugh
I see them gazing at each other
in adoration
Then I look at us.

I see her stroking his head when
he is feeling down
I see the bad times when they
don't make a fuss
I see her walk into the room and
pick up his frown
Then I look at us

I see them talking for hours as
though they've just met
I see him sending silly texts while
on the bus
I see them not letting anyone
become a threat
Then I look at us.

What Hurts Most.

It is what hurts the most in this
world and what can bring the
greatest joy.
It is what you dream of when
you are young; ideal girl meets
ideal boy.
But then you spent your whole
adult life looking for it.
You turn down many because
you are still looking for it.
It is so easy to base your life
search on misconceptions and
ideas.
For the time it takes to realise
the truth can take you many
many years.

It is always shown on TV and you
read about it in books.
But when you experience it in
real life it is not all that is looks.
You are filled with false images
as you watch the films or sing
the song
The hardest thing to handle is
when you find out they were all
wrong.

Once you find it, they say you are
lucky but it doesn't always last.
For most time you stay together
for habit, or for what you had in
the past.
What you thought you would
never do – you do, despite your
ideals before.

Life   Love   Spirit   Me

What you thought you would
never say – you say, as it changes
your perception more.
But when you are right in it, you
are the happiest person alive.
Your voice has a swing to it, you
walk with a certain stride.
The world is suddenly not such a
bad place...as you have someone
of your own
You have this feeling of inner
happiness, and you don't feel
alone.
It is love that gives a sense of
belonging - even if for a short
while
It is love that, despite all the
pain, can always make you smile.

Love can be confused with lust,
loneliness and bring about
feelings untrue
If you compromise your feelings
of real love it may come back to
haunt you.
Love hurts and it can hurt the
most when the love is not
returned.
When they say 'I love you back'
is it the same love that is
yearned?
In this life it is the most pure,
natural and beautiful thing.
But in this life love can turn you
mad and lead to retribution and
sin.

Who do you love? What is love?
Does it happen when your heart
feels that dip?
Is there that 'one special person'
for us or is it a point of, 'working
at the relationship'?
Love can keep your head in the
clouds until pain wakes you up
with a shove
It doesn't matter how much joy
it brings, what hurts most in this
world is love.

Man loves a woman.

When a man loves a woman, he
will find that she
Always knows the way to bring
out the best in he.

When a man loves a woman,
deep in his heart
He will impress at the end as he
did in the start.

When a man loves a woman, he
will recognise her beauty
Through all the days of her life
though others may not see

When a man loves a woman,
though he may try to resist

Life   Love   Spirit   Me

He cannot control the emotion
his feelings will persist

When a man loves a woman, he
will want to make her smile
Whether is to buy her flowers or
complement her style

When a man loves a woman,
through all the stress of the
world
She will be his one weak point
where all his problems are
uncurled

When a man loves a woman she
will show the another point of
view

And when the picture seems set
she will show him something
new.

When a man loves a woman, the
love will never end
When a man loves a woman
she's like no other for she is his
friend.

Spirit

A prayer

Each time I wake I want to aim to
be,
Unaffected by how people
regard me.
To give and not to expect in
return.
While others live, I want to live
and learn.
Oh I pray that my soul will never
grow,
To only think about myself and
what is my own.
To face my fears without being
afraid.
To be wise when decisions need
to be made.

Each day I wake I want to aim to
be,
In touch with you as your in
touch with me.
To ask questions and not follow
the crowd.
To be silent in voice but in heart
loud.
Oh I pray that I will always live
my life,
Without hatred in my heart and
without strive.
To try and understand though I
am not understood,
Instead of judging others actions
bad or good.

Each day I wake I want to aim to
be,

Life   Love   Spirit   Me

Whole in mind and soul and in
body.
To reach many height whilst on
the ground.
To count my riches in my spirit
and not in the pound.
Oh I pray that as I grow I'll never
seek,
To put down others perceived to
be weak.
To be strong in myself not to
compromise,
What is real in me for the things I
visualise.

Each time I wake I want to aim to
be,
A reflection of all the things
you've done for me.

Life   Love   Spirit   Me

To give and not to expect in
return,
What is given to me I will gladly
wait my turn.
Oh I pray lord that when we
finally meet,
I'd be worthy to be seated by
your seat.
And should I make some falls
along the way,
Your love will guide me back to
your pathway

Route to Brixton

Religion is like a bus route to
Brixton
We all have a route of our own
The problem is, we all think our
route is the best
And of others we are quick to
condone.

These different routes go
through different places
We tend pick up the bus close to
our way
Like to Buddhist man in China
Or the Hindu man in Bombay.

The bus numbers to Brixton take
different routes

Life   Love   Spirit   Me

Different ways of travelling the
same map
Different bus routes suit
different people
But this same different creates a
war gap

For the problem is all of the
fighting
With religion splitting friend
from foe
Both, forgetting why they are on
the journey
And the buses remain at the
depo.

But it's not the bus that gets you
to Brixton

Or the route you chose on your
way.
It is what you do when you are
on that journey
And it's God that has the final
say.

So if you are on your own bus
journey,
And you see another bus pass by.
Don't judge, condemn or
compare to your own
For, in Brixton you'll be asked
why?

Death will confirm

Every life takes a different
journey, but it all ends up the
same
Whether you take your life
seriously, or play it as a game.
Some walk alone on this journey,
some others need a friend
If we get to grips with life early,
the shock of death won't be the
end.
The bad decision that you make
in life – you have to live and
learn
Whatever you think was a
mistake in life, death will surely
confirm.

Everyday we gamble with chance
whether it be taking or giving
All hoping to advance to a better
conscious living
The situations we are born in can
determine the life we lead
But we must use the tools we're
given to build in what we can
succeed
Some chances you take by
yourself, can cause others great
concern
If cursed poverty or blessed with
wealth, death will surely confirm

Today there are many beliefs but
no one definitely *knows*

And sometimes when consumed
with grief this faith suddenly
goes
Is our loved one watching still?
Can we soon meet again?
Is it only those with good will
that can take a place in heaven?
Each religion preaches a
different thing but for the same
outcome yearn
For the uncertain questions that
life may bring death will surely
confirm.

Faith Part I

Living without faith is like
carrying water in a bucket with a
hole.
No matter how hard you work, in
the end there will be nothing to
account for.
Seal the hole before you carry
water – Seal your faith and it will
take you far.

Faith – Part II

Lack of faith is like going to war
without any armour.
Faith is the armour that protects
you
Stand for something in life, so
you don't fall for anything in life.

Ignorance is like going on a
journey with no food.
Knowledge is the food of your
life journey
You don't have to eat but you
won't finish your journey
without it.

Hate is like a cancer that spreads
through your whole body in time
If you truly love then you can
never hate.
If you let it, the cancer of your
heart will consume your soul.

From ashes to beauty

Lord of all this I pray
To be close to you day to day

Take me from ashes to beauty
What is dead inside Lord please
revived in me.
Raise me to honour from
disgrace
I know in your presence I shall
not lose face.

Give me from lacking to plenty
An abundance of you to fulfil me
Promote me from failure to
success
The past was a lesson with you
I'll progress.

Life   Love   Spirit   Me

Teach me to try and not to judge
I've been wrong and you don't
bear a grudge
Lord of all this I pray
To be close to you day to day.

Show me friendship from enmity
As you are the closest, dearest
thing to me
Enlighten me to joy from sadness
You bring me joy and for that I'm
blessed!

Lead me from defeat to victory
Let my losses bring out the best
me
Untie me from bondage to
freedom

Life   Love   Spirit   Me

Let me be free to praise you in
your kingdom.

Change me from my morning to
rejoicing
Death is life we should be
rejoicing
Lord of all this I pray
To be close to you day to day.

Karma

Fly by night and gone by day
'You are just to fast', all the girls
say!
Because you cannot let a single
girl walk by
Without the roaming of more
than an eye!
One day you meet a girl and
she's not the same
So you get her number and this
time remember her name.
Then things start to blossoms
and you fall in love.
You forget all the others because
you are in love...

But you call one night and she
doesn't answer the phone.
Instead the voice asks who you
are and the voice is deep in tone.
You've always use protection,
but you've lately had this itch,
When you get the connection,
know that karma is a bitch.

Chief Pastor of your church,
holding sermons thrice a week.
You spread the word of the Lord,
and only small payments you
seek...
All your friends and family are
just as faithful as you.
But you do not associate with
those that don't believe as you
do.

Life   Love   Spirit   Me

For thy shalt not kill,
Thy shalt not steal
And thy shalt not will themselves
on to what is others.
But you judge with a fate,
Those you perceive 'not great'
It is not God that creates, you as
he did your brothers?
Otherwise you live life as a 'good
Christian', but you are shocked
one day,
When you son you call Richard
now want to be called Renée.
Now love for your church or for
your son - you have to decided
which,
You've judged many now judge
one - because karma is a bitch.

Seen as a fool, when she went to
school
That African girl would sit at the
front in class.
So you would beat her, scorn if
you meet her,
And take away her bus pass.
She was trying to fit in 'trying to
be white', but she would need
more than just high grades.
And while your hair was slick and
tight, her hair was in nappy
braids.

'Black' is bad when 'Black' is cool
- but 'Black' is a past tense,
For 'Black' will be forever under
rule, if 'Black don't have no
sense'.

Life   *Love*   *Spirit*   *Me*

Now you have seen her, in her
Bema. Driving past as you collect
your dole.
You turn the other way, apology
at bay,
As the pride hardens your soul.
One thing to remember as your
schoolmate is getting rich
That knowledge is power and
karma is a bitch.

The perfect man

At day break I woke up by the
light of day
I knelt down on my knees and to
the Lord I pray
Please send me a man who is fair
in face
His love will be beauty to make
my heart race.

The Lord said:
If you knock I'll answer, you'll
find what you seek
You'll have what you asked for
by the end of the week.

So he sent me a man, tall and
handsome

Life   Love   Spirit   Me

So much was his face is held
beauty to ransoms!
But I was not aware this man
was secretly active
He left me for another that he
found more attractive.

At noon the sun was high, I
began to feel the heat
I asked the Lord to send me a
good man, a man that wouldn't
cheat!
A man that is honest, caring and
virtuous
As long as he loves me I will not
make a fuss...

The Lord said:

If you knock I'll answer, you'll
find what you seek
You'll have what you asked for
by the end of the week.

So The Lord brought me a man
was honest and true
This me could do anything he
just couldn't be bother to!
As loving as he was this man was
incredibly lazy
He couldn't make up with me so
our future was hazy

In the evening the long day
caused my heart to tire
I prayed to the Lord send me a
man I could admire

A man strong, ambitious with
intellect
Of whom I can rely, love and
respect.

The lord said:
If you knock I'll answer, you'll
find what you seek
You'll have what you asked for
by the end of the week.

What I sought, I found, a strong
man with confidence
With a mind of his own, yet he
was oozing arrogances
While I was a shrub he was the
great oak tree
After too long in the shade he
didn't even notice me!

Life   Love   Spirit   Me

Night time, quite time a time to
contemplate
As I speak to the Lord of my
choices of late
I will ask you one last time Lord
as you are yet to refuses
But this time oh Lord, this time
YOU CHOOSE!

Getting over it.

Please help me be strong please
don't let me call
Please help me be strong please
don't let me call
What he did was wrong and I
gave him my all
Please help me be strong please
don't let me call

Please keep me busy so I don't
think of him
Please keep me busy so I don't
think of him
I know he doesn't miss me 'cos
the phone doesn't ring
Please keep me busy so I don't
think of him

Life   Love   Spirit   Me

Please help me stay sane for my
life must go on
Please help me stay sane for my
life must go on
While me heart searches in vain
to find where I belong
Please help me stay sane for my
life must go on

Lord please.....

Shadow

Follow me in my life like a
shadow does in the day...

As day break becomes dawn, be
the light that guides my way

In the morning rise high, stay
close, teach me and let me
shadow you

At midday move to the side
within arms reach, what you
start let me continue

Late afternoon be near to watch,
walk with me over smooth and
rocky roads

Life   Love   Spirit   Me

In the evening when I begin to
tire, please help me carry my
loads

At night be one with me,
stronger than ever, presence felt
though not seen without light

When it comes for me to sleep,
as you rose with me in the morn,
fall with me at night.

The Meeting

On the day I meet the Father,
and I am standing with Him face
to face,
If He asks me what I did with my
life, how will I answer His grace?
Will I tell Him I was waiting for a
better day to bring out a better
me?
Will I tell Him I spent so much
time looking, that when it came I
couldn't see?
How can I explain I was too busy
living life, to sit back and think of
my role?
How do you explain you are too
busy feeding your body, you
forgot to feed your soul?

Life   Love   Spirit   Me

If He asked me, in the life I lead,
what joy to others did I bring?
For it is not only in actions but
thoughts and words can make
the spirit sing.
Will I tell Him I was waiting for
His consideration to bring out my
considering mind?
Will I tell Him I spent much time
thinking, that when it came I left
it behind.
How can I explain I was too busy
thinking of my life to think of the
life of others?
How do you explain being too
busy crying about your life you
forgot about your sisters and
brothers?

If God asks me, in the life I lead,
what lessons did I learn?
For this world is full of questions
with what answers did I return?
Will I tell Him I was waiting for a
wise man to teach me wise
things in hand?
Will I tell Him I spent much time
seeking, but when the answers
came I didn't understand?
How can I explain I was too busy
listening to false words, I didn't
hear Him I my heart.
How do you explain you were
too bust revising theories that in
the end you forgot the start?

If I was to meet The All and I'm
standing with Him face to face.

Life   Love   Spirit   Me

What will I tell Him I did with my
life, how will I honour his grace?

Things I need to do.

I need to wake up each morning
with a smile on my face
I need to tell the Lord I am truly
grateful for my time on His place
I need to take time not just join
the rat race
These are a few things I need to
do in my life.

I need to stop watching others
and start watching me
I need to be in touch with myself
holistically
I need to undo these chains and
let my mind be free
These are a few things I need to
do in my life.

Life   Love   Spirit   Me

I need to be complete in myself
so I can begin to help others
I need to do more than just
'understand' my sisters and
brothers
I need to have one good man
and not many bad lovers.
These are a few things I need to
do in my life.

I need to live as a free spirit and
not a tortured soul
All my weaknesses in life- I need
to take control
I need to understand why and
not just fulfil a role
These are a few things I need to
do in my life.

Life   *Love*   *Spirit*   *Me*

I need to lead a life that will not
cause others pain
To think about what they will
lose not what I will gain
If I don't do this in my life I've
lived it in vain
These are a few things I need to
do in my life.

When I die.

Don't cry, when I die.
Not every soul had the chance to
live as I.
Your life may not be certain- but
death is no lie.
In life we make choices, in death
find out why.

Don't weep, when I finally sleep.
For the memories we have we
will always keep,
And we will meet again when
you make that leap.
You learn more of life when you
finally sleep.

Don't morn when I change form.
I am present in the new world
where my soul is reborn.
The sun sets at night and still
rises at dawn,
Energy cannot be destroyed it
just changes form.

So please don't morn, but rejoice
when I die.
If the sun still rises than why
can't I.
If you speak to me I'm sure to
reply.
So there is not need to morn or
cry.

You

As you brought my beginning I
will see you to the end
For you are my mother my sister
my friend

When I'm down you don't pick
me up
But you offer your hand should I
choose to stand up

When I'm lost you don't point
me the way
But you show me a map so the
route I relay

When I'm confused you are not
my guide

Life   Love   Spirit   Me

But we weigh out the options so
I can decide

When I'm in the dark you don't
switch on the light
I learn to see with out my eyes
and you show me real sight

I haven't got wings but you've
taught me how to fly
And before I ask the question,
you've already taught me why

Now I fight fire with water and
show love where there's pain
If I am the heart you are the
artery and the vain.

As you brought my beginning I
will see you to the end
For you are my mother my sister
my friend.

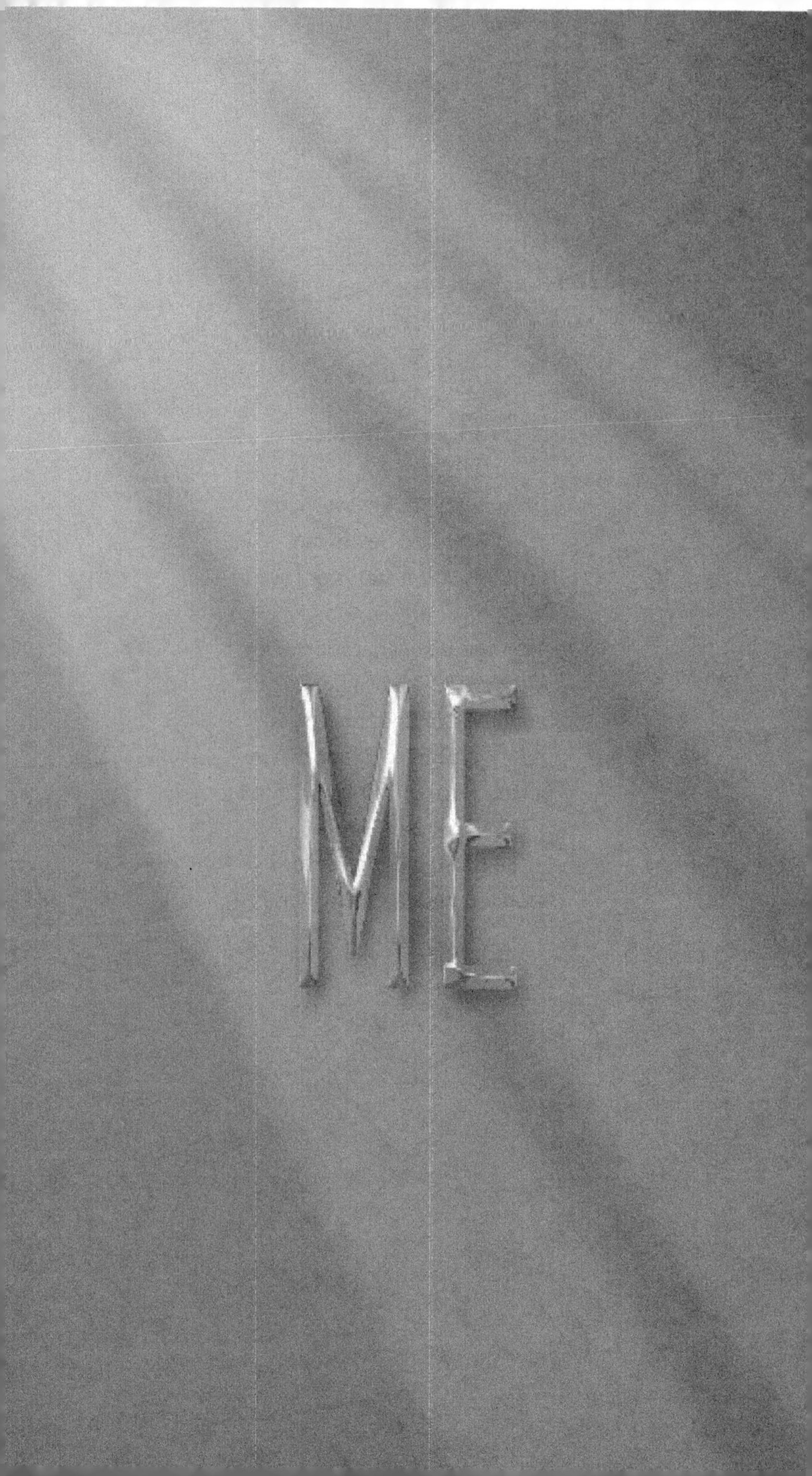
ME

African British Black

Too 'black' to be British, too
'white' to be African
Is this my social status as I live in
Britain?
I am the first generation of an
African line.
All my life in this country, still I
am yet to define,
A true place of belonging that I
can call home
So between two worlds I
wonder, between two worlds I
roam.

When I'm in Nigeria I am called
the 'white girl'
I don't live with their struggle I
don't live in their world.
Britain is a struggle, kept low, but
still trying to rise,
Where politically correct words
act only to disguise.
In those equal opportunities
forms, that claim to be
indiscriminate of colour,
Should I tick 'Black British', 'Black
African' or 'Black Other'?

It seems I am not fully African to
be classed as Nigerian
Yet no fully British to be
accepted in Britain.

Some people are dismissive of
their African heritage
They would rather live their daily
lives as English born and bread.
But like a lion in captivation
brought from the jungle, raised
in the zoo.
The lion doesn't truly belong
there or belong in the jungle too.

I'm part of a new generation of
the African, British black.
Not British enough to stay here
or African enough to go back.

Black brother of mine

Black brother of mine, where did
you go?
Can you not feel how much we
love you so?
Can you not see we are there
when times are low?
Black brother of mine where did
you go?

Black brother of mine why do
you fester?
You are a true king but you act as
the jester.
Buy the cologne stop using the
tester...
Black brother of mine why do
you fester?

Life   Love   Spirit   Me

Black brother of mine when will
you learn?
The times that we are going
through are causing concern.
Though this tough love may
cause you leave us inturn.
Black brother we love you when
will you learn?

Black brother of mine, where did
you go?
Can you not feel how much we
love you so?
Can you not see we are there
when times are low?
Black brother of mine where did
you go?

Close your eyes

Close your eyes.
Are you happy?

If you are to date, you have
achieved a state that many have
never reached.
Pastors have preached, and
mothers still teach; but for many
it is still out of reach....

Happiness is individual, although
it includes many
And if it your happiness doesn't
include any,
How did you get there on your
own?!
Are you happy, but alone?

Life   Love   Spirit   Me

Is your happiness a disguise?
Again, close your eyes.

If you are not
(Happy that is).

Only you know the reason why....
Is it a secret or lie?
Think of the part takings you
have had, in making you
perpetually sad....

Be close to the things that make
you smile
Turn the smile to a laugh that
will last for a while
You can get there on your own.

Life   Love   Spirit   Me

You're not alone.
You have the answer let your
spirit rise.
Again, close your eyes.

Dark

When the sun has set, when the
sun has gone,
And it is dark all around were the
sun once shone.
Dark is what I am, dark is who I
be.
Dark is the atmosphere that
completes me.
Dark is how I'm skinned, for dark
is in my genes
Dark is the colour of our previous
kings and queens.

When I'm tired I close my eyes to
remain in the dark,
It brings a sense of calm to the
troubles that I embark.

Life   Love   Spirit   Me

Dark is the blanket that keeps
me warm inside
Dark is the place of comfort in
this world that I reside.
Dark in solitary, silent and strong
Dark is the mystery, the place
that I belong.

When I sleep at night I sleep best
in the dark
My body remains dormant while
my mind is a spark.
Dark in a state of mind that
guides me in my dream,
When all is unsure in life, dark
remains supreme.
Dark is my light forward, dark is a
secret power

And dark is the entity that will be
in our final hour.

Anything deemed negative has
been related to dark
Anything deemed evil is branded
with that mark.
After this association, look at the
colour of my skin
What colour would you call me?
With what are you associating?
Dark is not any more 'bad' than
good is perceived as light
Still association of these terms
can't be withdrawn overnight.....

**We were once much greater
than this.**

Kings and Queens Rulers of our
own destiny
Once we ruled with our spirit
while others ruled violently
Our knowledge was power, their
ignorance was bliss
We were once much greater,
much greater than this.

We gave up the great in us, to
resume to great in them.
Still not aware that our greatness
is the originator of men.
Now everything we are involved
with, we are at the bottom of
the list

Life   Love   Spirit   Me

But we were once much greater,
much greater than this.

Realise we are all equal but we
are all not the same.
Today it is our group that is
losing the life game
For we will never get anywhere if
everything of ours we 'diss'.
Cause we were once much
greater much greater than this.

It is not money or intelligence
but unity we lack
Divided we fell but together we
can stand back
It has been written in history but
we still dismiss

That we were once much
greater, much greater than this

Cornrow

Mama please don't plait my hair
too tight
It hurts me when you do.
I always dread that Sunday night
When you call me to sit by you.

Those wide-teeth combs are not
wide enough!
As you pull and tug at my hair
Your excuse is that my hair is
'tough'
But the pain is beyond compare.

You comb and brush every
strand on my head
Then you comb and brush again
My scalp is sore and my eyes red

Life   Love   Spirit   Me

But my protests are in vain

Small and thin, you don't like
them fat
And no matter how much I have
resisted
I can feel every inch of every
plait
I feel hairs I never knew existed!

All week I hope you forget
Sunday night
And my hair I try not to mention
Because mama you plait my hair
too tight
Worry alone gives me
hypertension!

But if I stay still when you say
and bend low
If all your instructions I have
abided
I end up with a beautiful head of
cornrow
All neat and evenly divided……

But mama please don't plait my
hair to tight
It hurts me when you do.
I always dread that Sunday night
When you call me to sit by you!

I have a father.

I have a father aged 1.

Proud, kind man, intelligent and
strong.
First to teach me many things,
what's right and what's wrong.
Not afraid to work hard and
support his family.
He holds me when I cry and
feeds me when I'm hungry.

I have father aged 9?

On the pedal stool I placed him
and held him so high
So why did he leave me without
saying goodbye?

Life   Love   Spirit   Me

So why did he leave? Was there
too much pressure?
Without a word, a call or a
goodbye letter.

I have a father aged 17??

Was it something he ate, or
something in the water?
To make him walk out - stop
caring for his daughter?
I realise I'm not alone, there is a
common trend today
Were men are having children
and just walking away.

I have a father aged 23…..

I don't know where he is, not
sure where he has gone.
Why am I suffering when I have
done nothing wrong?
Now I am older it is all becoming
clear,
That if he really cared for me he
would be right here.

I have a father

Funny - many men have kids but
not many kids have a father.
Man enough to make a baby, but
in the end you would rather
Leave when times get tough,
while the family suffer on
But the repercussions of you
leaving will carry on and on.

Life   Love   Spirit   Me

I want to be me.

I look at myself and sometimes
hate what I see
I watch passers by walking, and
wish anyone was me….

At 41, ex husbands – three and
children – none
She is thinking of the past, the
present and what is to come.
She is thinking about the hard
lump she found in her breast
She is thinking how the last
chemo cycle did not make it
regress.
She is thinking if she had children
they might be able to support
her so

Life   Love   Spirit   Me

She is thinking of all the money
she has, yet alone she goes for
chemo....

———————————

"Beautiful lady," a young girl
makes a comment to herself
"I bet she has never needed a
dime plus she looks a picture of
health!

"While I'm a mother of 5 at 25
and reliant on others income
None of my family are alive and
my husband can't get a job
done."
She is thinking of her kids each
one is like their dad
She is thinking of the money now
she really wished she had

Life   Love   Spirit   Me

She is thinking of the bed-sit she
has to call a home
She is thinking as the banks
reject her requests how can she
get a loan...

_____

Young and carefree, oh what it
would be to be a young again!
I'd travel the entire world if I was
young and then I'd travel again!

"At 72 no one notices you and
only believe half the things you
say
Though your mind is alert it can
only hurt, them thinking you are
past your heyday
He is thinking of the months or
years he would like to relive

Life   Love   Spirit   Me

He is thinking when his body fails
will his mind still be active?
He is thinking when funerals out
weigh weddings, will he be the
next in line?
He is thinking how life can be
over at 72 when my mind feels
29?

_____

Can't wait to retire, working to
expire, to be old like the man
sitting there....
So content in himself, his own
divine wealth, just sitting,
breathing the air.

"I'm a young man living for
tomorrow, but held society of
yesterday

Life   Love   Spirit   Me

Because I don't follow the
perceived norm, I'm victimised
for being gay
He is thinking what how happy
he would be, living with no
inhibitions
He is thinking of the family that
love him, just under certain
conditions.
He is thinking if he tells all he is,
what is the worst that could
occur?
He sees a wealth woman without
a care in the world... and wishes
he were her.

Ihuoma

From an Igbo name meaning
'Good face'
You are the good-luck fortune
God blessed upon this place.
The beauty of your 'Ihu' only
hides your beauty within,
Of all the people in the room -
the most understanding.

Because you listen, when you do
speak, everyone heeds you,
Yet unaware of how you inspire
and affect what others do.
You bring luck to all around, with
your calm and positive self.

Uplift the spirit, and what comes
with it, is an essence greater
than wealth.

Strong enough not to follow, yet
you do not chose to lead,
You are the strength behind the
force of everyone indeed!
Understood by few but loved by
all, cause you have an inner
grace
That picks people up when they
fall; the mystery of your good
face.
May the love you give others be
returned 10 fold!

IHUOMA.

Late!

I'm still in bed and it is half past
eight,
Today I know I'm going to be
late!!
I'm rushing so I might leave on
time,
I'm still rushing and it is quarter
to nine!
Should I run for the bus or wait
for the train?
Please let me *never* be this late
again.
Maybe I should turn back and
call in sick,
That'll be my option if the train is
not quick....
Late train, bad traffic.... Is there
another excuse?

Life   Love   Spirit   Me

What can I say that will be of
better use?

Why is it, when you are late or in
a rush,
You are behind an 'L' plate or on
a slow bus?
Why is it, when you are late
everyone is going slow,
And you cannot overtake just
slowly follow?
Why is it, when you are late your
boss catches you walking in,
While all the time you are early
there is no one noticing??

Oh my goodness, another day in
vain,

I cannot believe that I am late
again!!

Music

Music consoles me
Almost controls me

Helps lift up my mood
Is my soul food.

Music makes me think.
Strengthens my weakest link

Reopens my vivid dreams.
When all's not what is seems

Touches my inner heart
When I think I'm falling apart.

Music comes with me
When I'm feeling lonely

Life   Love   Spirit   Me

Another person's expression
Brings out my regression

Relays my inner thoughts
Into words and all sorts

Music gives me ideas
When unsure and facing fears.

Music rhythms soothes my mind
In a world that is cruel and
unkind.

Music gives me hope
When I feel I can on longer cope.

Music makes me believe
That romance will never leave

Music holds history and future in
one.
But right now, in life, music is
fun!

When things fall apart.

I'm falling, falling and falling very
fast, I can feel myself slipping
away.
I'm running the race and coming
last and there is nothing I can do
or say.
Somebody help me- no one can
hear me, too busy in their lives
to notice.
That I'm hanging on and on
desperately, and cannot take
much more than this.

These thoughts rule my head and
slowly consume my heart,
This is how I feeling take over me
when things fall apart.

Life   Love   Spirit   Me

How did the decisions I made
come to this? Where did things
turn for the worst?
Was there a warning sign that I
did miss, or is it simply that I am
cursed?
I cannot control the actions of
others, but others seem to be
controlling me.
I am frowned upon by my fellow
brothers, and I am too proud to
say I'm sorry.

It seems the choices I made were
not very smart,
This is how feelings take over me
when things fall apart.

I know all things are not as bad
as they seem; but I want is to
crawl in a hole and hide.
I want to wake up and find this
was a dream, and no one
recognises me outside.
We all take risks, which are ours
for the choosing, our decisions
could be wrong.
But it is not winning the race but
how we handle losing, that
separates weak from strong.

So I get up, brush down and go
back to the start,
For I will not crumble when
things fall apart.

Heaven

Heaven is
The bright night stars as clear as
in the day
The smile you leave with
someone, as you walk away.

The air conditioning in the car at
noon
The innocent excitement of
Christmas coming soon.

The kick back on the sofa after a
day's hard work
Or settling into a hot bath
because your whole body hurts.

The rush you feel as you get
closer to your goal
The pay check you receive, after
years on the dole.

Heaven is
The tears of laughter in your
mother's eyes
The look of love she gives that
cannot be disguised

The quiet of the night when all is
silent and calm
The elderly couple still walking
arm in arm.

The intimate thoughts between
two heads that lay

Knowing that he loves you more
than he can convey.

Silent words across the room
that only you can understand
The elderly couple still walking
hand in hand.

Heaven is
Waking up early to see the sun
rise
Having no one you hate, wish
bad for or despise.

The relief you feel when all the
work is done
Looking to the future and
knowing the best is yet to come.

The tingle inside, when he calls
your name
Knowing that he loves you and
you feel the same.

The voice that sings the exact
words you feel inside
The friend for many years in
whom to trust and confide.

Heaven is
The place your spirit goes when
you body is at rest
Knowing that God loves you and
that you are truly blessed.

The first bite of a meal that you
have been craving for

Life   *Love*   *Spirit*   *Me*

A compliment from someone
you haven't met before.

Lying in on Saturday morning
and watch Saturday TV
A thank you for something you
do naturally.

Although in small doses, is
present here indeed
Heaven is today because
tomorrow is not guaranteed.

Words

Words are...

A writer's music
An ignorant lesson
A rapper's hope
A poet's expression.

Thoughtsfull

'Thoughtsfull' is a collection of thoughts in the eyes of a London born Black-British teenager. She describes in varied thoughts and perceptions that have influenced her as she matured in years.

Now a grown woman, the once guarded words of 'Thoughtsfull' is realised by the author for her full thoughts to be shared.